P9-APN-126

DANCING DILEMMA

BOOK SERIES

Published By

OHC Group LLC
PO Box 7839, Westlake Village, CA 91359

TM & © Copyright 2005 by OHC Group LLC. All Rights Reserved.
www.onlyheartsclub.com

SECOND EDITION
ISBN 0-9763213-1-9

Printed and bound in China

The Only Hearts Girls™ formed
The Only Hearts Club® in a bond
of true friendship. They are a fun-
loving bunch of friends who are
always there for one another. They
laugh, share secrets and have the
greatest adventures together. Most
importantly, they encourage one
another to listen to their hearts
and do the right thing.

Contents

Karina in Ballet Class

Karina Grace stood tall and poised at the ballet bar. Her teacher, Madame Dubeaux, pushed the PLAY button on the CD player, releasing a stream of violin music into the room.

"First position," Madame Dubeaux said, clapping her hands. Karina touched her heels together and pointed her toes out to the sides. Her head was high and her arms curved gracefully at her sides. She glanced at herself in the mirror and smiled. Her pretty blond hair, which she usually wore down, was up in an elegant bun, the way she always wore it for ballet. Karina's blue eyes sparkled. She felt so happy when she was dancing. Every twist and turn and leap tickled her bones. Karina was especially happy about this class because one of her best friends, Briana Joy, was in it, too. The two girls shared something else special – they were members of the Only Hearts Club, a fun-loving group of six girls who were always there for one another.

They laughed, shared secrets and had the greatest adventures together. Most importantly, they listened to their hearts and always tried to do the right thing – even though it wasn't always easy to do.

As they stretched next to each other on the bar, Karina asked Briana, "Do you like the class?"

"Well, I guess it's OK," Briana responded, as her curly brown hair bounced on her shoulders. "I like sports better, but since soccer season is over, dancing is a fun way to hang out with you and the other girls."

Karina's take on dancing was completely different. She lived, breathed, ate and slept dancing and music.

Madame Dubeaux clapped her hands again. "Second position. Third position…"

Karina moved effortlessly through the poses. She practiced each of them at home in front of her bedroom mirror every evening. She loved the way her legs lengthened when she walked on her toes. When her arms were a perfect oval around her head, she smiled, thinking about how she looked just like a real-life version of the tiny ballerina twirling in the music box in her bedroom. Karina lost her train of

thought as someone brushed close by. It was Hannah Faith, who, as usual, wasn't posing correctly.

"Lift your left arm a little," Karina whispered helpfully to Hannah.

Hannah felt a little embarrassed. "Oh, thanks," she said. After a quick run-through of the dance sequence Madame Dubeaux had choreographed, the girls gathered their belongings and headed home.

"Briana," said Karina, walking on her tiptoes on the sidewalk next to her friend, "I feel bad for Hannah. She's nice and I think she really likes ballet, but she doesn't seem to be doing very well."

"Well, you have to remember that dancing comes naturally to you," replied Briana. "Some people take longer to learn. I did notice that Hannah does better when you're dancing in front of her."

"You mean, she copies me," said Karina proudly.

"Yeah, that seems to help her remember the positions," agreed Briana.

"You know, I bet with a few extra lessons, Hannah would do really well," said Karina.

"Maybe," said Briana when they had reached her

house. "Well, I'll see you tomorrow."

"Bye!" said Karina. She pirouetted and spiraled toward her house. She had a good idea for tomorrow!

Helping a Friend

After rehearsal the next day, Karina caught up with Hannah in the dressing room.

"Um, Hannah," she began. "I…uh, noticed that your pirouettes were really good today."

Hannah stared back with her eyes wide open. "Are you kidding?" she asked. "I thought they were really bad."

Karina tried to hide her smile. "No! No, they weren't, really. You, um, maybe just need more practice."

"You think so?" Hannah asked as she slipped her tutu into her bag. "I don't know. I'm much better at hip-hop. My pirouettes look more like pretzels."

"So did mine once," giggled Karina.

"Well, even if a few more lessons is all I need, my mom will only pay for these classes with Madame Dubeaux, and they're almost finished."

Karina hesitated, staring at a cracked tile in the floor. "Maybe I could help you," she said.

"Really?" said Hannah excitedly. Their eyes met and they smiled.

"Yeah, why not!" said Karina. "Come to my house on the days we don't have rehearsals."

Hannah was so happy she jumped and twirled all the way out of the dressing room and the dance studio.

"Well, it sure looks like you made someone's day," said Briana as she and Karina watched Hannah dance out the door.

Exciting News

After only a few special practice sessions with Karina, Hannah's stance had already improved. Her pirouettes were tighter and her leg extensions nearly flawless.

"You're a good teacher, Karina!" said Hannah. "Madame Dubeaux is tough and sometimes she makes me kind of nervous. But with you, I feel like I can do anything!"

Helping Hannah made Karina feel good, and she smiled.

During the next rehearsal, Madame Dubeaux moved Hannah to the first row, next to Karina! Karina felt so proud she thought her heart would burst! Hannah looked nervous about being up front for the first time, so throughout rehearsal Karina kept looking over at her, nodding and giving her a "thumbs up" sign to let her know she was doing well. Hannah soon wore a smile so big that every single tooth showed.

Suddenly, their teacher waltzed over to the CD player and turned down the music.

"Now, class, gather around," Madame Dubeaux said. "As you know, this year the ballet school is putting on its annual production of *The Nutcracker*, one of the best-known ballets in the world. Because you are now a year older and more experienced, you are all eligible to audition for a part in it. We will be holding auditions in a few weeks, and one lucky young lady will be selected to dance in the production later this year!"

Many of the girls in class shrieked with excitement. They had dreamed of performing in *The Nutcracker* ever since they started ballet. Now they would finally have the chance!

"These flyers list the schedule of tryouts and performances," Madame Dubeaux said. As the excited girls reached out their hands for a copy of the pink flyer, they looked like baby birds stretching their necks to be fed by the mother bird. "I think a certain number of you should consider it," Madame Dubeaux said as she glanced toward Karina...or was it Hannah?

A quick flash of heat shot through Karina's stomach.

Well, Hannah is getting better, thought Karina, *but she's not that good yet.* Karina relaxed, chalked her emotions up to excitement over the auditions, and forgot about it.

Madame Dubeaux unclipped the stack of flyers from her clipboard and handed them to the class. "If you wish to try out, please come prepared to dance a short audition piece of three minutes or less," she said. Soon the girls were streaming out of the dance studio to share the exciting news with their parents!

"There's my mom!" Karina called to Briana, and the two friends raced over to meet her. Before they had even put on their seatbelts, Karina had relayed every last detail about tryouts for *The Nutcracker*. As her mother started the car, Karina noticed Hannah and her mother talking by the curb.

"...And Madame Dubeaux thinks I could get the part!" Karina heard Hannah tell her mother.

What? thought Karina. *I'm the one who's supposed to get the part!*

No Worries

"What part will you be trying out for?" Karina's mother asked her that evening. But Karina didn't hear her. "Why don't you ask your sister to help you plan your audition piece? She can accompany you."

"Mmm-hmm," Karina said absent-mindedly. Karina's older sister, Monica, had been taking piano lessons for six years. Maybe with her help, Karina could put together a really wonderful audition piece.

After dinner, Monica sat at the keyboard in the family room to practice the piece for Karina's audition. After listening for a little while, Karina leaped up and ran to her room. Her feisty dalmatian, Dotcom, was at her heels, barking playfully. As Karina practiced her pirouettes in front of her mirror, she could see Dotcom standing on her hind legs and hopping in a circle behind her.

"Well, aren't you a special dog!" Karina laughed.

Dotcom made a noise like a giggle and wagged her spotted tail. Karina jumped and stretched until it was way past her bedtime. Before long, Dotcom grew tired and stretched out for the night in her dog bed next to Karina's bed.

"Good girl, Dotcom!" Karina said as she put on her pajamas and got into bed.

Why was I so worried about the audition and about Hannah? thought Karina as she drifted off to sleep. *After all, I taught her!* With that worry out of the way, she could hardly wait for the audition!

Competition for Karina

Ever since Madame Dubeaux had mentioned the audition, Karina had been especially focused in class. She wanted to be in *The Nutcracker* so badly, she even wore her best tights and pinned her hair back in an extra-tight bun for rehearsal. She daydreamed that every rehearsal was the real thing, imagining she was center stage with the spotlight following her every movement.

Madame Dubeaux clapped her hands and Karina snapped out of her trance. She and the other girls stopped stretching on their own and took their places at the bar. Madame Dubeaux turned on the music and commanded the girls.

"First position," she called.

Karina swept into it skillfully.

"Second position. Third position…"

Again and again, Karina's body transitioned fluidly.

But she noticed that Hannah's poses looked great, too, and Madame Dubeaux, who usually followed Karina's moves in rehearsals, was now looking – no, *staring* – at Hannah!

Suddenly there was a loud *thud*! The girls froze in their positions, but their heads whipped around to find Karina on the floor!

"Is there a problem, Karina?" Madame Dubeaux asked, frowning as if she had just discovered a bizarre object she hadn't seen before.

"No, Madame," Karina answered quietly. Hannah and Briana unfroze and went to help Karina to her feet.

"Uh, thanks," said Karina sluggishly.

Madame Dubeaux changed the music and herded the girls into three rows in the center of the floor.

"I have a new step to show you," she said. She stood with her ankles together and extended her wrist forward as if beckoning someone. "Hannah, would you come front and center, please?"

Hannah! Karina couldn't believe her ears! Madame Dubeaux had never called anyone but Karina to the

front when explaining a new step. Suddenly, all the air seemed to have left the room. All the sound, too. Karina felt as if she could hear a pin drop. The planets had seemingly fallen out of alignment.

Despite the fact that Karina was not up front, out of habit the girls focused on her instead of on Madame Dubeaux and Hannah. Karina looked as if she were frozen in place.

Hannah was so surprised and nervous to have been called that she hadn't noticed Karina's expression. When she looked toward Karina for one of her reassuring "thumbs up" signals and instead saw Karina's look of shock, Hannah suddenly realized what had just happened.

From the second row, Briana cleared her throat and coughed on purpose to break the silent tension in the room. Karina gathered herself and seemed to thaw a bit. She tried desperately to look encouragingly at Hannah, as though having Hannah up front had been her idea as well as Madame Dubeaux's. After all, Karina didn't need the spotlight *all* the time.

Advice from Friends

Walking home after rehearsal, Karina and Briana passed the park where they sometimes met their friends to play with their dogs or ride bikes. The other Only Hearts Club girls were already there, playing with their dogs. When Karina and Briana joined them, Karina relayed the details of the ballet rehearsal.

"Isn't that the girl you helped with her ballet steps?" asked Taylor Angelique, tossing her dark blond hair.

"Yes," answered Karina with tight lips. "How could she do this to me?"

"It doesn't sound like she did anything to you," said Anna Sophia.

"But…"

"Look, Karina, you know you're the best little ballerina in the whole town," said Olivia Hope. "And it sounds like you've been a super helper, too. So what's the big deal? Practice your steps like you always do and I'm sure things will work out."

"Well, I guess. But I didn't think…"

"…She would get better than you?" Lily Rose finished.

"Yes," Karina said as she lowered her head.

"Personally," said Anna, "I don't see what's wrong with having two great ballerinas."

"The problem is there's only one part up for grabs for *The Nutcracker*," Karina answered.

Briana put her hand on Karina's shoulder.

"Look, the audition hasn't even come up yet," Briana said. "Maybe Madame Dubeaux was trying to be nice and encourage her."

"Maybe…" Karina said, but she didn't sound very convinced.

Hannah Gets Nervous

There was only one week left until the audition, and Madame Dubeaux was teaching them a whole new sequence. The girls stepped into position and the music started. Madame Dubeaux posed herself in front of the long mirror and danced out the sequence. All eyes were on her as the girls made mental notes of the steps. When she had finished, she played the music again and called out, "Five, six, seven, eight…"

The girls danced the sequence as best they could.

"Well done, ladies," said Madame Dubeaux. "Now, let's go over some steps from *The Nutcracker*. The auditions are coming up, and I want those of you who are trying out to be very familiar with the steps." At the reminder about the audition, Karina stiffened. She was really getting excited and working hard, but she was still nervous about how Madame Dubeaux seemed to be praising Hannah as much as she was praising Karina.

The rehearsal went well. Afterward, Hannah followed Karina to the dressing room.

"Good rehearsal, huh?" she said.

"Any rehearsal where I don't fall is a good one," said Karina. She couldn't help but smile.

"Karina, I know you're practicing really hard for the try-outs and that we're going for the same role, but do you think you could still work with me?" Hannah twirled the sides of her skirt in her fingers. "I've never auditioned for anything before. I'm so nervous."

Karina thought for a moment. She had, after all, offered to help Hannah in the first place, so she couldn't just say "no" because Hannah had gotten better. That would be shallow – something the Only Hearts Club could not tolerate. Still, Karina wanted that role. She had been dreaming of it for years, and a few weeks ago Hannah wouldn't even have dreamed of trying out for *The Nutcracker*.

"Sure," said Karina cheerily but a little reluctantly. She thought how nervous Hannah got, and how extra nervous she would be for the audition.

They worked together for four straight days, and

Karina pushed Hannah to do her best. After their last session together, Hannah had some questions.

"How many people are at an audition?" she asked Karina tentatively.

"Oh, lots. The judges, all the girls from all the classes…" Karina began. She noticed that Hannah was cringing slightly and had an uncomfortable look on her face. Karina decided to go a little further. "…And sometimes the boys come from their basketball practice in the gym and watch, too. Lots of times they laugh at us and make comments about our ballet outfits, but it's nothing to worry about."

Hannah looked like she had a stomachache all of sudden. "That's a lot of people watching us, huh?" she asked. "Well, how strict are the judges?"

"Oh, they're OK," said Karina, as she put her CDs in her bag. Hannah didn't see Karina looking at her in the mirror. "As long as you pick the right kind and color of ballet outfit for the audition."

Hannah's brow knitted. *How could one possibly know that?* she thought. "What else should I be worried about?" she asked.

"Nothing, as long as you don't make any mistakes during your audition," Karina said. Then, as if she suddenly remembered something, Karina started again. "Well, except the floor."

"What's wrong with the floor?" asked Hannah.

"Well, the floor on the stage where they do the ballet auditions gets really slippery," Karina fibbed. "So if you start to fall, lean backwards so you don't land on your face!"

All these things made Hannah extra nervous. And Karina knew it.

"The audition's tomorrow, so get some rest tonight, OK?" said Karina somewhat guiltily when Hannah's mother came to pick her up.

"Thanks for everything, Karina!" said Hannah, and she threw her arms around Karina's neck, hugging her so tight she almost choked her. "You're a good friend!"

Karina's heart felt heavy in her chest. Hannah darted off, but just before she hopped into her mother's car, she stopped and glanced back at Karina. Hannah looked nervous, and it seemed she wanted to say something to Karina but couldn't. So she just swallowed hard and copied Karina again and gave her a "thumbs up" sign. Karina smiled back, but it was only a little smile. Something didn't feel right about what she had just done to Hannah.

Karina Listens to Her Heart

That night, Karina tossed and turned in her bed. More than once, Dotcom came over to see if she was OK. Karina had been so worried that Madame Dubeaux might choose Hannah for *The Nutcracker* that she had tried to make Hannah extra nervous for her audition. She knew that wasn't nice, especially since Hannah trusted her. And to make it worse, Hannah had still been so nice and thankful, even after Karina had tried to make her nervous. Karina tried to shake the bad thoughts out of her head. She tried to focus her mind on the fact that a role in *The Nutcracker* was the important thing. But she couldn't forget what she'd done to Hannah. Karina knew she had taken advantage of Hannah's trust and inexperience for her own benefit. She had done the wrong thing. That wasn't what a member of the Only Hearts Club was supposed to do. They had all agreed to think with their hearts and to try and do the right thing. Before she

31

drifted off to sleep, Karina decided that tomorrow she would do just that – *before* the audition.

The Audition

It was the day of the audition, and the auditorium halls were buzzing with excitement. Adults were milling about with clipboards, and girls were stretching in their crisp leotards. Some were twirling and some were biting their fingernails out of nervousness.

Karina wasn't nervous at all. She was ready. But first she had one thing to do.

"Hi, Hannah," Karina said after she found her friend in the girls' dressing room.

"Oh, Karina, I'm so nervous," said Hannah, whose hands were visibly shaking. "I don't know how I'm going to do this. I've never been on a stage alone in my life, and from what you told me, this is going to be really difficult."

"Hannah, I have something I have to tell you," Karina said slowly, looking down at the ground and shaking her head gently. "There's really nothing to worry about."

"But you said…" Hannah started.

"Forget what I said," Karina sighed, looking at Hannah. "The judges are puppies, the floor isn't slippery at all and if the people make you nervous, just picture them in their underwear." Hannah laughed. But then she stopped and looked at Karina.

"But then, why did you tell me all those awful things about the audition?" she asked.

"I guess I was a little jealous that you'd gotten so good, so I tried to make you more nervous," Karina admitted as she again looked down at her ballet slippers. "Can you forgive me?"

Hannah didn't answer with words. Instead she hugged Karina. "Thanks for admitting it. That took a lot of guts, and most people wouldn't have done it. I'm not mad at you. How could I be? After all, if it weren't for all your help, I wouldn't even be here in the first place!"

"Really?" Karina asked. She flashed a little smile at Hannah. "Thanks. And good luck, Hannah. You've worked hard, and you deserve it as much as I do. If I don't get the part, I hope you do."

Hannah smiled. "Ditto," she said, and they hugged again.

Just then an announcement came over the loudspeaker. The auditions were about to start. The girls darted backstage.

When Karina peeked around the curtain and saw her friends Taylor, Briana, Anna, Olivia and Lily in the audience, she felt a surge of happiness.

Karina volunteered to dance first. She walked gracefully to the center of the stage, posed with her left leg forward, toes pointed down and her arms in an oval above her head. Her head was tilted downward, but she knew exactly where the spotlight was above her. She waited for the music to begin.

When Monica played her last note, Karina knew she had danced flawlessly.

Hannah was up last, growing more nervous as she watched the other girls. Though her routine was quite different from Karina's, she danced equally well. It seemed like hours before the judges made their

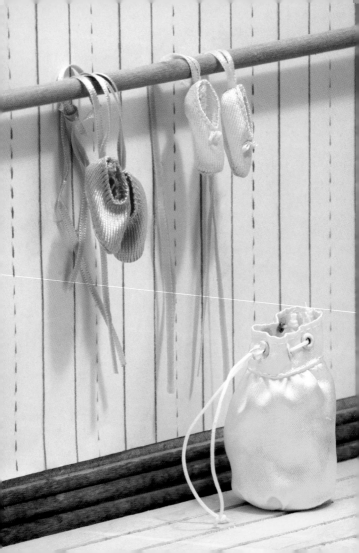

decision. Finally, they assembled all the girls on stage. Hannah and Karina held hands and squeezed tight.

"I want to thank all the girls who auditioned today," said the judge. "You were all very well prepared and danced beautifully. I wish we could ask all of you to join us in this year's production of *The Nutcracker*. Unfortunately, as you know, we are able to take only one young lady from this class. We are pleased to announce that the role for our production of *The Nutcracker* this year goes to…" the judge paused, "Hannah Faith!"

Karina's left hand went limp and fell from Hannah's grasp. Karina wanted to run off the stage and hide. Instead, she caught the eyes of her fellow Only Hearts Club members in the audience and turned to Hannah and shook her right hand.

"Congratulations, Hannah," she said and left the stage quickly. Hannah was speechless.

Surprising News

The next week, Madame Dubeaux had begun a new session of ballet classes, and because Hannah had done so well, her parents had agreed to pay for her to continue. During the next rehearsal, Madame Dubeaux again called Hannah to the center, but this time she caught Karina's eye and winked at her.

Karina did not know what that wink meant, but something about the twinkle in her teacher's eyes reassured Karina. After class, when all the other girls had left, Madame Dubeaux called Karina aside.

"I'll catch up with you in a minute, Briana," Karina called as she jogged toward her teacher. "Yes, Madame?"

"Karina, I just wanted say how proud I am of you. I know you've been helping Hannah." She put a hand on Karina's shoulder. "And I know how much you wanted that part. You created your own competition, but you didn't back down when the stakes got high.

You danced your heart out. And you lost graciously. That's the mark of a true professional. You are a special girl and a special dancer."

"Not special enough for *The Nutcracker* though," Karina said with a sigh.

"My dear," Madame Dubeaux smiled, "When we share our gifts with others, we don't lose them; we just make them grow stronger."

"If that's true, then why didn't I get the part in *The Nutcracker*?" asked Karina. "And why did you single out Hannah in class?"

"Because I wanted you to get inspired. You are the best dancer in the class, but if you aren't challenged, you won't grow." Karina felt Madame Dubeaux's arms encircle her in a hug. "And you've grown tremendously over the courses. That's why I was saving another role for you."

Karina looked up for the first time in the conversation. "But there was only one position and the judges gave it to Hannah."

"For that performance, yes." Madame Dubeaux said. She led Karina to the set of chairs where the class kept their backpacks and Madame Dubeaux kept her CDs and folders. She slipped a sheet of paper from her bag and handed it to Karina.

"This is the schedule for the real *Nutcracker* that the city ballet performs downtown," said Karina as she scanned it quickly. Her eyebrows narrowed, and then, as if someone had pulled an invisible string on the top of her head, Karina's eyes and mouth flew open.

"You mean…" she hesitated, not daring to believe that it could be true.

"Yes, dear," said Madame Dubeaux, who had been struggling to hide her own excitement until the perfect moment. "You will be dancing in the performance on November 28th!"

"What?" Karina nearly screamed. "Really? The *real Nutcracker*! I'm going to dance in a performance of the real Nutcracker? But that's only a few weeks away. How will I…?"

"I've already spoken with your parents and they've agreed to the rehearsal schedule," Madame Dubeaux said, no longer hiding her enthusiasm. "It's just one performance and it's a small part. One of the young fairies in the city ballet has to go out of town that night and you're going to fill her spot. What do you think of that?"

"I...I..." Karina began, but the lump in her throat wouldn't budge. She wrapped her arms around her teacher's waist and squeezed with all her might.

"Karina, you've worked so hard. Just as you helped Hannah, she in turn helped you. You may not realize it, but you've blossomed into an even more phenomenal dancer. You were too focused on Hannah to notice."

Karina pulled away from her teacher and flashed a big smile.

Sleepover

Sleepover at my house this weekend!" Karina announced to her friends from the Only Hearts Club after school the next day.

When her friends arrived, they placed their sleeping bags in a circle around a plate of popcorn and fruit. Pretending something bad had happened, Karina began talking in a low, flat tone to get her friends to quiet down. But she couldn't contain herself for long and blurted out her incredible news! They were all so excited for her!

"And by the way," Karina said to her friends. "I think we may have a good person to join the Only Hearts Club!"

"Who?" asked the other girls together.

"Hannah Faith," replied Karina. "She's a really sweet and forgiving friend. I know she appreciates kindness and doing the right thing, so I think she'd be a great addition to the club.

"Let's invite her to our next sleepover," Lily suggested.

The girls nodded and smiled.

The Performance

The night of the performance with the city ballet was exhilarating. Once again, Karina peeked around the curtain and saw her family and friends sitting in the audience. Even Hannah was there with that big smile that showed all her teeth. Karina smiled at Hannah and waved. She was happy for her new friend, and Hannah was happy for her. As a matter of fact, shortly after the audition, Karina had warmly congratulated Hannah on getting the role. Hannah had given Karina all the credit and offered to return the favor by giving Karina some hip-hop dance lessons! Hannah was a great hip-hop dancer, and Karina was excited to try something new – especially since it had to do with dance!

The lights dimmed and the curtain opened. The first few scenes seemed to take forever. Finally it was

Karina's time to dance. The music swelled and Karina and the other "fairies" glided across the stage. Even though she was in the back and her scene lasted only a few minutes, dancing on that stage felt like an illusion to Karina. Was she really dancing with the city ballet company in a performance of the famous *Nutcracker*? She pinched the back of her hand when she pirouetted just to make sure she wasn't dreaming!

Although she had been on stage only a few moments, they were magical moments that Karina would cherish forever.

I listened to my heart and did the right thing, all on my own! she thought to herself. *That felt really good and made everything work out for the best. It's cool to do the right thing!"* And what a grand reward she received for it! She couldn't wait to talk to Hannah. After all, she had a lot to thank her for.

~ DANCING DILEMMA ~

Read all the Only Hearts Girls' heartwarming storybooks.

It's Hard To Say Good-Bye
When her friend loses her dog, Taylor Angelique finds a new puppy for her. But will Taylor Angelique keep the cute little puppy for herself?

Horse Sense
Olivia Hope's horse develops a slight limp right before the big show. Will she go for the blue ribbon or choose to save her horse?

Dancing Dilemma
Karina Grace is the best dancer in school. Will she let her talent get in the way of her friendships?

Teamwork Works
Briana Joy is a superstar on the soccer field. Will she try to win the game by herself or be a good teammate and help a friend?

Two Smart Cookies
Anna Sophia's pie is ruined just hours before the big bake-off. Can she whip up Grandma's secret recipe in time?

Peep for Keeps
Lily Rose discovers a lost baby bird in the forest. Should she keep it as a pet or return it to nature?